ISBN: 978-1-960157-26-3 (Paperback)

Title: Frank the Frenchie and the Christmas Tree Hunt

Author: Meg Lindemulder

1. Children's Books

FIRST EDITION

Cover and Illustrations: Anna Semenova

Published by Bookfox Press

Printed in the United States of America

I dedicate this book, and many more to come, to my incredible husband. The word "supportive" doesn't even begin to describe this man. He works tirelessly as a firefighter, picking up overtime shifts, so I could quit my corporate job and follow my dreams of being an author. Brandon, you're my best friend, and I adore you beyond words.

SHOULDA COULDA WOULDA

Frank the Frenchie and the Christmas Tree Hunt

Written by Meg Lindemulder

Illustrated by Anna Semenova

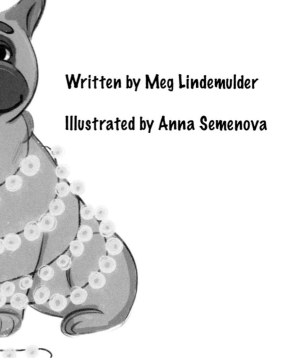

"Just like last year and the years before,

we'll put on our warmest coats and scurry out the door!

With mittens in our pockets, we'll find our tree,
then celebrate with cocoa—that's a guarantee!"

"HOORAY, HOORAY!" Frank jumped with cheer...
but one thing was certain: he wasn't wearing
that silly coat like last year.

The coat had bright red and green reindeer
from head to toe,
with a big Santa hat attached that read, "Ho, ho, ho."

Frank's family ran frantically out the door,
and with squinted eyes Frank threw his coat
on the floor.

"This one will do just fine,"
Frank proudly said to himself,
as he grabbed his spring jacket from the very top shelf.

"Wait for me," Frank shouted,
joining the others.
He was certain he'd be just
as warm, without looking silly –
unlike his brother.

As the family approached
the Christmas tree farm,
Frank and his mother skipped arm in arm.

Frank's mother stopped skipping
and zipped his jacket up to his throat.
"Frank, why aren't you wearing your warm winter coat?"

"It's silly and bulky and goes to my knees!
I don't need to wear it
to look at Christmas trees!"

After hours of searching, Frank's ears began to sting.
Wishing he'd brought that winter coat
he was told to bring.

"That one right there,
that's the one I admire!
Now let's head back
and warm up by the fire!"

"That one right there, with branches that are bare?
Don't be silly, sweet Frank—we must choose with care!"

The freezing winter air blew down Frank's neck, and he realized he'd gotten himself into a wreck.

As he shivered head to toe, he began to think twice.
That silly winter coat would sure feel nice.

"I'll meet you by the fire,"
Frank shouted at last...

...as his family cut down the perfect tree,
having a blast.

As Frank was wrapped in blankets with a cold, runny nose,
Frank's family skipped inside and proudly struck a pose.

**Frank's family cheers'd hot cocoa in their mugs,
then rushed over to Frank, giving him lots of hugs.**

I SHOULDA

listened to my parents' advice
and wore that silly winter coat
in the snow.

Then **I COULDA**

been warm out in the cold
and helped pick out
the perfect tree to tow.

Then **I WOULDA**

been all snuggly and warm to celebrate with my family and some hot cocoa!

About Frank

This book was based on a real French bulldog…my furbaby, Frank! Frank is hilarious, so loving, and always entertaining. He always finds himself up to no good, but he can get away with just about anything with that sweet face. He enjoys swinging at the park with our human baby, Callum (Cal). They are the best of friends.

Author's Note

With a shiny new Journalism degree in 2012, I had no idea what the world held for me. Long story short, I found myself at a crossroads after 12+ years in corporate America, staring mindlessly at a sales screen 40 hours per week—which I consider taking the very unscenic route in life— came the year 2020, and it was COVID. The world was shutting down, and I finally had spare time to write!

My French Bulldog, Frank, was just a pup at the time and always had me laughing… and running around. He was playful, adorable, and highly rebellious. I opened my laptop, and my fingers went to town; my creative juices—as I call them— were in full force. Before I knew it, I found Frank concluding each story in the common phrase, "Shoulda, Coulda, Woulda."

Frank always goes against the suggestions of others and thinks he knows just about everything. So naturally, Shoulda, Coulda, Woulda became the bread and butter of all 12 stories that I ended up writing.

I am incredibly passionate about writing, poetry, and storytelling. I adore children and the precious way they view the world. Similar to Frank, the innocence of a child can often lead to lessons learned…lots of lessons! Luckily, stories in this series will teach your children valuable lessons in an extremely exciting and loving manner.

 I truly cannot wait to share this first book with you all, and please know there will be more releases to come!

XOXO!

Made in the USA
Monee, IL
13 December 2023

49107207R00021